Horsemouth and Aquariumhead

Horsemouth and Aquariumhead

Elizabeth Horner Turner

BLACK LAWRENCE PRESS

Black Lawrence Press

Executive Editor: Diane Goettel
Chapbook Editor: Lisa Fay Coutley
Book Cover and Interior Design: Zoe Norvell

ISBN: 978-1-62557-149-6

Published 2024 by Black Lawrence Press.
Printed in the United States.

Table of Contents

Horsemouth and Aquariumhead

THE WOMAN WITH the horse mouth sighs; she tries delicately, but with that mouth, whatever comes out is a snort. Her gait is even rather equine—her head posts up and down as she strides. She is waiting for the man with the aquarium head—no further instructions other than *you'll know him when you see him*, and if he'd been given any instructions about her, they'd be the same. She doesn't know what an aquarium head will look like—rectangular with attachments? Like the treasure chest at the bottom of a tank? But when he finally arrives, she knows. His head is green-tinted glass, like something found on the beach, and beautiful. He's filled with water weeds, wavy grasses, fish darting about, and behind all that is a pair of moony human eyes. She whinnies, trying to portray a sense of recognition and excitement, but she knows that all he probably sees are her yellowing teeth. He takes her hand and leads her away. *I am walking down the street with a man with an aquarium head!* she thinks, and then wonders how he breathes. When he turns his head to look for cars, she sees the pink gills flapping behind his ears. She blushes above her horsey snout and shoves a sugar cube in her mouth. She wonders how he eats, and where they are going.

The man with the aquarium head takes them up a hill and down another to a bench overlooking the city; smog curls around the middles of buildings like tutus. She is sweating a little and bends to drink from a hose placed to fill a communal dog bowl. Then he hands her a book—*Spells to Counteract*. He pats the seat next to him. On a small pad of paper, he writes, *how did it happen to you?* and pushes it towards her. The woman with the horse mouth ruffles the pages, sighs again, and dollops them with greenish spit. *Work. Jealousy*, she writes. *I dated the boss. I didn't know there were witches there*. The man with the aquarium head nods and writes again, *Everyone was a witch? No*, she scrawls. *Just two. A man and a woman. We had a company performance of A Midsummer Night's Dream*. Bubbles pop at the top of his head as he starts to laugh. The woman with the horse mouth begins to laugh, too; she whinnies and snorts. *They didn't even get the right animal!* The man with the aquarium head reaches into a pocket and pulls out a canister. He shakes it at his new friend. Standing up, she unlatches the top of his head, and the greenish glass sparkles in the sun. She sprinkles in flakes of food. The bench is in the shade and the city fuzzes in the late afternoon. She knows just when to stop.

The Road of Dead Frogs

YEP—

It's me again. Remember that time you asked me what the worst thing I encountered in my Research Job was? I didn't really have an answer then, so I brushed off your question. I was also trying to kiss you, and talking about my job probably wouldn't have helped. But I know now. The worst thing was a plague of frogs. Well, that's what I call it, anyway. There was this one night. I was driving to the site and the last stretch of road was filled, I mean absolutely crammed, can't-see-the-asphalt jammed up— with tiny frogs. All on top of each other. When I put on the high beams, all I could see was their little, wet-looking bodies hopping so slowly in this massive, froggy traffic jam. There must have been thousands of them that night, clogging the back road that was my only way to the survey spot. I sat in the car for a while trying to think of what to do, and I couldn't think of anything. I just had to keep driving through them. So I did, and it was horrible. I heard their little bodies squish and pop under my wheels. It was foggy too, and so noisy with all their croaking and my old car's engine. I didn't see anyone else on the road, and about two minutes in,

I was convinced I was losing my mind. When I finally got past the plague and to the site, I could still hear their muffled croaks haunting me. I heard them all night long.

That was four years ago, but I still have freaky dreams about it. Ones where I've been in standstill traffic and each car around me is driven by a frog, and ones where I wake up naked and covered in them. I have no doubts that my afterlife will involve some kind of service to amphibians: never-ending fly catching for their meals, granting freedom to those waiting for dissection, or maybe even being eaten alive by a frog over and over like a swampy Prometheus. There's just not much I can do to make up for that awful night— I mean, what was I supposed to do? Tell the government, "Sorry I can't make it to your high-security research site to do my super-duper important job, but I don't want to hurt the itty-bitty froggies on the road?"

I know I should have. I know.

But anyway...here I am—still showing up at our bar for Happy Hour every other Thursday, still nursing a Magic Hat like a stoned '90s college student, and I'm still writing these letters to you while also maneuvering my laptop away from puddles of beer. I just can't make myself find a new place, even though this one bought a karaoke machine during your absence to "liven things up" and it makes me want to die. And it's because I can't accept what is likely true—The Secret that happened to you that no one can talk about; The Secret that I can't even write about in this note because somehow, my computer will be hacked and They'll find out that I Know and I'll be Secreted Away, too. I've gotta admit, though— that possibility sounds better and better these days.

I do love you, you know, even if I'm bad at showing it. When

I write platitudes like "I look forward to seeing you"—I actually mean what's implied by that phrase—when I imagine being with you, I get an adrenaline slam in my stomach and goosebumps all over my arms. Every single time. This little folder here, my virtual hole behind the brick behind the painting, is getting more and more stuffed with these notes.

Next time I write—I'll try it. I will. I'll write in explicit detail why I think they've taken you and where to and see what happens. Maybe if I hadn't gone to work that night, killing all those frogs, and I'd just met you at the bar like you pleaded with me to, I could have saved you. And the frogs. It could have been more than this. More than this apology. And we could have tried another beer.

Simply Not a Disaster—

I AM STILL here, the crash just a feathery echo now, and my shadow darts about when it should be dabbing my wounds and helping me up. I wish I could get this letter to you, darling, dearie, sweet pea o' my heart, because then I could continue to torment you as one does in the shoulder-tapping, neck-kissing way of those with our type of relationship. The type we bought after agonizing together at Home Depot. You wanted the motherload of ornate cabinetry and me, I wanted the bowl sink, the sink with hammered, metally depth to catch our water like wooden buckets did for old-timey hand pumps; I was so enamored with *Little House on the Prairie*. So we got both. Both! They raised their eyebrows at the relationship checkout stand, but our plastic cards had enough numbers and we looked ready. We were ready.

But this crash really tosses a wrench in, doesn't it? If my shadow would just wipe away this bloody pool that's collecting, maybe push aside some of the wreckage that has me trapped, I could mail you this letter. At least I have the healing process to look forward to—a quiet, clean place with antiseptic-smelling people knocking knees and taking pulses. Big windows and airy light puffing through curtains. Perfectly smooth enamel water pitchers, starched linen sheets. There'll be a woman in the bed next to mine, and she'll tell me her story before she finally goes, and you and I will spend the rest of our lives sharing it so everyone will know that she was a fighter. I may look a little wan now, but I'm not washed out quite yet.

I'm over near a tree, a big live oak, and it's been long enough since the crash that birds and squirrels have started creeping back. One sat on my chest, its head cocked with that look birds get that either means "I'm hungry" or "I'll listen." I took a gamble and asked the bird to please find you. Staring hard into her little brain, I sent the best message I could. I thought our address over and over; I thought about love and help and that it was all worth it; we were always all worth it.

I have to hope she's left to find you, perhaps peck-typing my message in mini Morse Code on bits of bark. She'll tuck those scrolls into her bird carrier leg brace and fly to you, complete with her own soundtrack. When she arrives, you'll read the note thoughtfully, strew some bird seed for her as a thank you, but she'll be off. You'll chew each bark bit to absorb my every word and come find me because that's the kind of person you are: a searcher.

When you find me, open my belly. This letter will be there, nestled among organs and bone. If someone gets my liver, darling, make sure you get this letter. It is for you.

— Your honeling, your heartbait, your dessert-in-the-wait.

Writing You From the Train to Mara, Hoping That You'll Care for Her—

BECAUSE IN THIS SLOG all I've got are the muddy boots and sloppy drinks and her mayonnaisey fingers.

Her finger smears on the window that cannot be undone by the breathe-out-and-wipe-the-fog method, and while this journey is easier, undoubtedly easier without her, she's still in her milk teeth and all that wet—

I miss her. I miss her, every gooey inch. But crazily enough, I am still going. Going to Mara for who knows how long, going because I must, I must for all the girls all over the world, for all the shadows down in our Afternow, and yes, for *us*-us, and because against every bone in my body—

I still wanted an OK from you to do it and when I got it, I had to go.

The office next to the carousel up in the hills is the only place one can still get train tickets to Mara, purchasing them beneath a leaky roof and eucalyptus trees and moldering piles of pigeon feathers. The ones to Mara are still written out by hand and let me tell you, this ticket seller is slow. Over an hour in line just to get to the front, but at least she writes my name in the thin, old-fashioned, spidery loops that I was hoping for after such a long wait. She spells it with a *ph* and not an *f* without me needing to tell her, and the seeds and such from her furtive snacking grace her wrinkles and dot her knuckles. According to her badge, her name is Ethel.

That moment made it all worth it—when she handed me the ticket—for at least the moment, anyway. Worth the damp and the muck, well, more than that of course, but let's not dwell on that.

I am en route now, chuffing along. I wish I could tell you what will happen when I get there, but all I can say is that it's Mara. MARA! A glint of ocean and wax stamps and the best kettles of tea ever. I hope to buy a new bathing costume when I arrive because that is what they should be called in places like Mara.

I love you, you know, even though to the best of my knowledge, I shouldn't. Check in on her, will you? The Little Plumpness. Crossing the river now and getting so sleepy. Wish me luck.

Wearing a Paper Bag Is One Kind of Hide and Seek

EVEN THE THREE year old managed to find her, no toes behind couches, no dust bunnies nibbling at the eyelashes of the hiding. She was just right there in the kitchen, breadcrumbs piling up around her tattered jeans—it's difficult to find your pie hole when you've a bag over your head.

"Ha!" said the kid, the little girl with smudgy fingers. "Ha! You're found!" and poked the bagged woman in her innards.

The crumby chewing ceased immediately; marmalade dripped in blips and blops down the plaid flannel shirt. When the bag was slowly pulled off, birds chirped and buds burst into flower on the plumeria bushes. The little girl felt like running, she felt like presents, she felt like this was a woman in need of a napkin. To this little girl, the velvety, felted sound of one creased bag pulled off one graying head was the sound of the angels in the christening books kept next to her bed. With it off, she could look at the woman's face. Her eye sockets were filled with marbles—cat's-eye and sea-glass green and multicolored, flecked ones bigger than the rest, those ones that always seemed like bullies. They shone and glinted and flickered. They clicked against each other. The mouth that belonged to the glassy eyes began to open, and the three year old slapped her little hands over her own face.

"You got me," the marble-eyed woman said, beams of light arcing over every crumb in the kitchen. "Now let's play some tag."

When she rattled her knees and thumped her heels, possums shot out from under the house like a gasoline fire. As the light hit the little girl's cheeks, she felt ready for anything.

"How 'bout I hide this time?" she said. "I'll give you my toast. My nice toast with banana slices. Maybe you need another snack."

"Eco-Friendly"

I WAS IN the car when the voices started. At first I thought the dry-cleaning bags were just stirring in the breeze from the open window, but the next time I picked up my dry cleaning, a bag grabbed my hand as I was hanging them up on the back seat hooks. I told myself this time that it was static cling; I wiped it off and drove away, but as I turned on to Sunset, the bags were definitely whispering. Murmuring together. My heart started to race, and I accidentally blew through a red light. Their voices started to grow louder and more clear—

"We know you hear us," they said. "Please listen!"

"What do you want?" I yelled and pulled the car over. Staring into the back seat, I heard the bags start to giggle that type of nervous laugh that people do sometimes. I was so freaked out that I let a scream rip and collapsed on the steering wheel.

"OK, OK. We're sorry," they said, sounding a bit petulant. "But we need to tell you something."

I raised my head and sniffled. "Alright, I guess. This is just really freaky. What—what do you need to say?"

Then the bags started talking. They told me about worker

mistreatment at the dry cleaners, about all the toxic chemicals used there, and that if a dry cleaner puts "eco-friendly" into quotation marks, it doesn't have to actually mean anything. The bags told me that basically all I've been paying more for is recycled plastic bags, and that the workers at this place are all slowly dying.

Well, I pulled my dry cleaning from that place pronto and started an investigation. I got decent social media traction and a reporter interested which helped expand my search. Then one day when I was passing out flyers about the toxic chemicals used at this one place on Broadway, a woman got into it with me and punched me in the mouth. Let me tell you—I went pretty wild then: I pulled her hair, kneed her in the kidneys, the works. Videos went viral, of course, but because she started it and called me a *hippie bitch*, somehow it got spun as "Soccer Mom Beats Environmental Activist" even though I'm the soccer mom and she's an oncologist or something. Anyway, that was the last straw for my husband—Wayne said I'd lost it and that my behavior made him afraid for our kids. After they left for school the next day, he packed me in the car to go spend a few weeks at a fancy Women's Retreat Center because I "clearly needed to get it together." And I hadn't even told him about the talking bags yet.

At first, I was lonely at the spa, but then I started to make friends because apparently, a lot of women are sent away by their partners. The kids came on the weekend, and it felt like the best vacation ever. We went swimming, snuggled in front of the fireplace, and they got their first massages. The rest of the time I had daily therapy and went on hikes; I got to eat meals that someone else made, and I took a lot of naps. The bags even sent me a couple of letters. I'm surprised I received them as their handwriting is terrible, but they told me that several dry cleaners were closed down after other folks took up my cause. The chemicals some cleaners used were found to be linked to different kinds of throat cancer. The bags said they were proud of me; that this movement wouldn't have started without me listening.

When I was allowed to return home, Wayne sat me down to tell me about a new software engineer. She started as an intern in the "Computer Chicks Rock!" program that partners female computer science grads with tech companies. She's been really present for him during this trying time, and he feels more connected to her than he ever did with me. He'll put me up in an apartment while we figure out the separation. He wants the kids to split time.

I had a helluva talk with the dry-cleaning bags that night—everything from blaming them to asking to be suffocated in the closet. They refused to do that, and somehow managed to lock the door to keep me out, but they continued to talk to me all night through the crack underneath. They said I was better off without him and reminded me of all the contacts I still had at my old company. That I had faked it almost every time with Wayne, even when he went down on me. That two terrible dry cleaners were now closed, and three others changed their chemicals to actual eco-friendly ones, because of my work.

My kids made me blueberry pancakes the next morning and told me how much the new girlfriend sucked. I'm pretty sure I said all the blah blah good mom in a separation junk I thought I was supposed to say, but I think they were disappointed. Later that day, I went to the closet to thank the bags and every single one of them was gone. Just gone. The clothes hung there, naked on their twisty metal hangers, saying nothing. So I started tweaking my resumé. I mean, what else was there to do?

Smalldom

THE YEAR I lived in the snail shell was a private one. Not lonely, no, but for me and me alone. It was beautiful. The sun when it poured through the shell, the opaque glow—it was heaven. I would knock on the sides with a tiny mallet to make music, race up and down, in and out of that golden spiral, and fling myself down on my rear end to shoot down the slick curves. It was fun. It really was fun. I ate grasses and leaf bits and gorged on acorns and sucked rotting fruit when I wanted a buzz. I played chicken with birds—lay just enough of my body outside the shell and was still and quiet until I sensed their quick dive down to pluck me up. I'd roll back in and feel the rattle of their missed snack.

It wasn't a choice, really. I woke up early one morning just really small. Tiny. Climbing over the pillows to lower myself into my husband's ear to tell him what happened took hours. He was kind, really; he cried when I told him I needed to be in the backyard.

"What will we tell the kids?"

"Oh, darling. I don't know. Let's not make this a drama, shall we? Tell them I am finally studying in Europe like I always threatened."

"I'm sure this can't last forever, right?"

He lowered me down into the flower bed I so carefully tended.

"Monday afternoons, I'll have Gerald come to fix up the garden. Stay out of the way of the mower."

That was more difficult than I imagined, but I got into a rhythm. Wake up on Mondays, scoot the snail shell into an ivy bed (Gerald never raked the ivy) and hang out for a few hours while my jaw rattled with the noise of the mower. Late afternoon, scoot snail shell back.

I only watched my family in the window sometimes. It was too hard—Laura bent over her books at the table, hair knotted around her finger; Thomas gaming on the living room rug, feet splayed out in front of him.

The day I woke up full size again, I wept into the lavender. The shell rested on my chest, faded and weather beaten, the white around the edges dry and flaky. The little fence around the garden crushed under my legs and cut into my thighs. When I rose up, I fitted the snail shell on my pinky finger and made my way to the back door. It wasn't until I was halfway up the stairs that I realized the door was unlocked. I kissed the shell and rested it on my nightstand. As I pulled my arm around my husband, he whispered, "You smell like lavender."

Yes. Yes. The garden.

Her Golden Zipper

YEARS AGO, a woman was banished to the house on the river because she was rumored to murder men. We all think it was likely a better place for her, anyway—so much magic abounds at the edge of every river. Some say she was an Amazonian who grew to a height of twelve feet tall when she was angry. They said that if a man did something untoward, she'd scoop him up and crush him in her jaws real quick. Some say no, that she was actually regular-sized, but her jaw unhinged like a snake's. Can you imagine the hours of agony, they asked, as she worked each body down her throat? Others think she used magic to shrink men down and fed them to whatever lived in the river. Some believed she sucked them dry and flew their skins like kites. But here's the thing: I think I know something closer to the truth. I know a man who was her lover and lived.

He says it all started when she asked him to feel her heart. He says that they loved each other but at some point, he wanted out.

"I was nervous," he told me. "You know, the relationship was going really well, so something must be wrong. I should get out, right? I know, I have issues. But when I told her, she actually seemed OK. And right before I left, she begged me to get inside her chest. I thought she was being metaphorical, trying to get me to really understand her, you know? Like—*get inside my chest* was *get inside my head.* But she wanted me to feel her actual heart. And after I got my brain wrapped around the sheer wildness of it all, I thought, yeah. Okay. I can do this for her."

So he agreed, and he said it was easy. She slipped out of her dress and tugged on this tiny golden zipper right in the middle of her chest, right on her breastbone; this zipper he said he had never felt or seen before when touching her skin. She unzipped, and he placed a couple of his fingers into the tiny opening and somehow, he got sucked right in. Right there, into her chest and straight into a ventricle. He said it was warm in there, and tight, but not claustrophobic. And the most incredible part, he said, was that surrounding him were all sorts of words he hadn't really heard her say before. Thoughts. They swam all over him, around his body and into his head and through his eyes. At first, the words were rough and painful as they penetrated, things about himself he didn't want to face. But as he started to really listen, he said it was like the best warm bath ever. Like pure, pure love tonic. He had never felt that safe before, he said. After a while, it got lonely in there, so when she was asleep one night, he climbed up her throat like a tickle and pulled his way out on her molars.

"I wanted to make her something," he said, "so she knew that I understood."

The villagers said her screaming began around six the next morning. They said she must have walked from the river because when they saw her, she was naked and covered in mud, scooping up anything she could get her hands on—dirty napkins, pigeons, coffee cups—and pressing them to her chest, trying to force them inside her body. They said she fought off four cops until she finally collapsed and was taken away. We haven't seen her since. And all the while, the man said, he was back at his house, knitting her a sweater.

The Contagious Circus

THE CONTAGIOUS CIRCUS is going bankrupt.

Duh. It's the name, of course, because who wants to come to a place that advertises contagion and disease? It's just that we promised her we'd keep the name—we promised her on her deathbed, because when else do sweeping promises get made like that, except to ease one another a little more gently into the hereafter?

So we promised our Forsythia, wasting away in her tightly sheeted bed, Forsythia, coughing all that sparkly blood into her matted handkerchief. We promised her we'd call it The Contagious Circus because she was The Founder, she was the First Believer, and she had The Magic. (She also loved alliteration and word play, which for most is simply a precious hobby, but in this particular case, it has caused us nothing but financial woes.)

So we're filing bankruptcy on a circus that promotes laughter.

Here's the thing: it's not even really a Circus circus—it's just simply unstopped magic. How it goes down is basically this:

- The audience enters through spangly doors and puffs of glitter.
- Cotton candy is handed out for free.

- Fireflies dim their lights, the insect band begins, and we appear on stage, each holding different glass bottles.
- One at a time, with our own personal flairs and announcements, we unstopper our collected laughs to the people.

As the audience hears the first one, the tent is almost always eerily silent. People never know what to do at the beginning, and there's so much running through their heads—Is there more? Is this it? Should we boo? But that's when it all begins to work, you see, and our dear, departed Forsythia knew it—the insect band, the glitter, the spangles, and our super-secret cotton candy recipe in the Perfect Portion Cups—it's all there to set up the Laugh Bottles and by about the third unstoppered laugh, the audience starts to roar! Tears ooze and feet stomp and babies wet themselves. (Some adults as well, which is why we have Comfortably Waterproof Cushions.) The Contagious Circus is simply a place to catch laughs.

We continue to believe that in this world, there is never enough glitter or laughter. So please consider coming to our final show this Friday evening—we're giving away free spangles to the first 25 guests.

Esther Jenne
and the White Hot Hearts

I STARTED A BAND called Esther Jenne and the White Hot Hearts, but then I had to learn to play bass. My hands are small and my pinky doesn't stretch well and the whole practicing thing was hard. I wanted the calluses to show I was tough, but the playing was painful. These days, my hobbies are metaphor and third grade assignments of I Used To, But Now...

I used to have desire, but now I have sloth.

It was a good time, third grade. I looked good, and I read the shit out of *Witch of Blackbird Pond*. I long for my lavender sweater with dark purple hearts, the one with the shoulders that kind of poofed up? I long for my homemade ribbon barrettes and my Strawberry Shortcake lunchbox. I long for the red plastic glasses with no lenses that my mom got me because I wanted glasses so badly, and I want my Zilpha Keatley Snyder books. I long for dust motes in the air by the live oak tree.

I don't think this is just a list about longing for childhood, though.

I remember losing that purple heart sweater one day during PE. When it was hot, I used to put all my jackets and sweaters and stuff on the orange plastic benches that edged the playground. So the other day, I ditched what I knew as my life and walked to find it. It took a while; I had to walk back through my teenage years all the way to that milk-stained playground where I began, and I've been here ever since. I didn't find the sweater, but I did begin my rock band, which is cool. And I think because I managed to nail down a couple of chords (despite my shorty fingers), and I'm good with facial expressions, we hammered out a few gigs. But I got lost living back here. I lost shoes. I lost direction.

We tried to find it together in a Meditation of our Inner Child class—me and the White Hot Hearts. They figured maybe they could use some help, too, especially since it was about time for an all-girl punk band revival, so we got the mats and the oils; we chanted, and we held hands. We even saw Life Coaches—all together and on our own, but then Marcy decided to become a nutritionist and quit the band. We're looking for a drummer if you know any.

So we posted the ads and the Life Coach recommended another Meditation Class where, after the first couple of meetings, we'd get to meet our very own Inner Child in a Safe Space. The Capitalizations helped us to Understand that This Is Serious.

I got on board. This wasn't a third grade assignment. I went deep and my feet fell asleep, and wouldn't you know, I found [me]:

I found [me] again with the bangs and the buck teeth and the ribbon barrettes and damn it! there was that purple heart sweater on [me]! When I went to hug myself at age seven, she looked me up and down and said, "Oh, I don't think so. I don't want to be... this."

She flicked her hands at me like I was a bunch of mosquitoes. Then she climbed to the top of the playground climber that smelled tinny like blood and stared me down until I opened my eyes in class and wept loudly and disturbed the whole room. Even empathic meditators kick noisy people out.

I used to want to meditate but now I think it's mean.

So I edged down the street like Little Miss Awkward with Calming Oils, all angles and neroli. I think I want to see [me] again, but back then I was a little scary.

I used to be all tough and honest, but now I feel like milk.

Oh yeah, and I don't care how much they make at those Life Coach jobs, I think they're a sham.

Baiting and Other Lures

YESTERDAY. A BOBCAT watched my dog pull and pull at the leash, and then walked backwards, its eyes on everything, especially the nose and tail.

Who is called to help with a bobcat vision?

Long ago. A small white dog at a rest stop bit a boy and a girl (well, just the girl). The girl bit the boy. Dogs can't bite two people at once. The bites above her kneecap swelled to electrical sockets while the owner cried and gave out band-aids and tubes of ointment. The boy was twenty-one, stoned, and looked at pictures of the grandchildren in the RV.

Is it best to duck and cover or give a bobcat stare down?

Life's not so weird here with bobcats. Why, we've got deer eating lawns and oak trees. I was going to run for it, but my dog decided against it. Then came this magic trick—the bobcat became a dog and followed us home, watched from the middle of the road to make us nervous, (big enough to eat us), and my dog ate a squirrel skin.

Is it more important to know who's killed first, or if the bobcat is real or not?

The boy, who took the blonde to a creek near the little white dog who bit, is a brunette. Later on in the same trip, he also took the blonde camping where she got 72 mosquito bites. They gave a night fisherman some views of sex near the lighthouse, and then she scratched her bites and infected her blood. More ointment and pills helped, but no one wanted her looking after children that summer.

The bobcat didn't bite because it was really a dog, you know.

The brunette who drove across the country, who watched a dog bite a girl, laughed afterwards because it's cruel and trite. But this can change—I'll be the brunette and she's still the blonde, remembering lightning bugs and a bike ride, a moon so big she rode to it. I'll wrap a towel around her legs and then we'll walk home to read weather headlines, "Stars Tonight. Clear."

But really.

The blonde got a neck-ache from staring out the car window and threw away music that wasn't hers when the boy stopped for coffee. Her leg throbbed. The dog had tags, but you never know. If I had been there, I'd have saved her from bites, wrapped myself in honey for the insects so her blood could pulse clean.

If the bobcat was a bobcat, I'd like to think I'd go first.

When The Girls Came Driving

WHEN THE GIRLS came down the street, it was always in a fleet of '70s muscle cars—sometimes rusted out, sometimes newly refurbished, but always matching. A parade of Firebirds one time, and the next was Mustang fastbacks. But this time, their last time, the cars were truly divine. The Girls drove a caravan of matching 1970 Chevelles—all chestnut brown and speckled with glitter. The stripes down the hoods were black mica, and the chrome burnt my eyes with its silver. To look at them was to be inside a star; those cars sparkled so intensely that the transformer on the corner of Blight and Wan blew as they rolled by. Those of us waiting for The Girls were showered in white and orange sparks. We cheered as flames licked the wires. George the veterinarian had a smoldering mustache. Celia, I swear, Celia had a halo of lights in her hair, and as they winked out, they didn't leave a single mark. She tells anyone who will listen that on that day, her scoliosis was finally cured. No one called to get the transformer fixed, because no one messed with an appearance by The Girls.

Usually, we smelled the shift in time before they arrived. The air would blow briny, a whiff of seaweed, a hint of dock rot, a taste of the center of the sun on our lips, and windows up and down the streets were thrown open. Women struggled into moth-eaten tube tops and Dr. Scholls sandals held together with duct tape; men girdled themselves into tiny shorts and old Sex Wax t-shirts. Sometimes people just came out naked, as naked with The Girls was always better than staying inside.

*The girls the girls the girls are here the girls the girls the girls have come thegirlsthegirlsthegirlsthegirlsthegirls...*the collective whisper built from our houses as we got ready; we couldn't help but say it out loud as we brushed our hair and searched for our Bonne Bells. We felt the engines first, the thrumming engines of their cars beat in our breasts as we primped and hurried outside. The cars evaporated clouds from the sky with their heat; the sun burned and gleamed off their paint jobs like fire. We'd woozily clutch each other and gulp in the biggest breaths we could, as though inhaling the leaded gas and smoke could trap their essence within us. It was The Girls, you see. We did it for The Girls.

As they drove by that last day, their hair flew out the windows, undulating like ribbons. This time their hair was from the sea— blue-green and salty; each Girl's locks flowed like waves. The cars left streaks of sand and tidepools behind them. Hermit crabs skittered along the curbs. As The Girls turned to smile at us, their skin shone with green-gold scales, and we saw the gills on their necks. Waving sinewy arms, flicking their tongues like serpents, we were enraptured.

And then something happened, something different. A young girl in a popsicle print sundress and braids—I hadn't seen her before, not ever—tore herself from her mother, ripping puka shells from her neck as she went, and raced up to the very first car. Even over the thrum of the engines we heard her yelling, "Take me! Please! I want to go!"

She launched herself at them. Her mother lurched forward to grasp one white sandal just as her daughter wedged her head and an arm through the passenger side window.

We all gasped. No one had ever dared to touch The Girls before. Pete, the man on the corner who tended his succulent garden with the care of a lover, yanked the mother back to the crowd. A voice made of gravel cut through the engine noise, hissing "Gloria, take the wheel!" and several webbed hands reached out of that first car, clawing to pull the young girl fully inside. Her mouth opened and her eyes closed as she collapsed, ecstatic, onto the vinyl seats, and Gloria gunned the engine. Their tires skidded down the street as the entire parade raced off, and in the last shower of sparks from the transformer, something hard hit my head. Rubbing the wet off my hair, I saw blood on my palm. A spiky seashell lay at my feet, perfectly formed, twisty and blue-green. The young girl's mother fell out of Pete's arms, clutching handfuls of sand and weeping. She was still in the street that night as we blew out our candles, one by one.

I kept the shell. By the next morning, some people began to say that The Girls were kidnappers and we should all lock our doors, and the girl's mother paced the streets of the city with a poster of her daughter in the popsicle print dress. We were out of power for a week after The Girls came.

When I can't sleep, which is most nights, I take out the shell to listen to the faint hiss of the ocean. I know they'll come back one day. I have the shell. Whenever I smell the sea or the rot, or I feel sunshine in my mouth like we did on the days The Girls came driving, I take it off my shelf. I haul open my window as far as it will go; I grab the boom box I bought at a garage sale and push play on my mom's old cassette of *Horses*. I blast "Gloria" as loudly as I can, *G-L-O-R-I-A*, and scream the only name that mattered out our front window, guitar and cymbals and Patti's voice a frenzy in my body. I call and I call for The Girls, for Gloria, to come back for me. I want to be saved. I want to know why they didn't take me.

Acknowledgements

MANY THANKS TO the following journals and anthologies for first publishing my work, often in slightly different forms:

Fairy Tale Review: "Smalldom"

Lost Balloon: "Horsemouth and
                            Aquariumhead"

PoemMemoirStory   "Wearing a Paper Bag
(now NELLE):   Is One Kind of Hide and
                            Seek"

Pumpernickel House: "When the Girls Came
                            Driving"

Red Mountain Review: "Baiting and Other Lures"

trampset: "Simply Not a Disaster—"

Best Small Fictions 2021:   "Horsemouth and
                            Aquariumhead"

Thank you to my friends, family, mentors, and students who have supported me over the years. Big, forever love to Chris and Terry Horner for decades of unwavering belief in my writing. Thank you to the English, Comparative Lit, and Creative Writing departments at Hamilton College for helping me to cut my writing teeth and providing generous mentorship. Thank you to my teachers, mentors, and classmates at Sarah Lawrence College as I bumbled my way through an MFA. Thank you Amy Glynn, Kate Oksas, Kelly White, and all my local editor friends and family. Kelly spent more hours with some of these pieces than was probably healthy, and I am in her debt. Thank you to Darcie Dennigan and Micol Hebron for being badass writers and artists who helped me be true to myself in my LA years, and who continue to inspire me even from miles away. Thank you to Rachel Richardson, David Roderick, and my fellow writers at LeftMargin Lit. What a special and important space!

The writing and music of Patti Smith and Santigold were my consistent writing and incubating companions these past several years. They're both deeply inspirational humans to me in many ways, and especially as they navigate the worlds of artistry and motherhood.

Thank you to Diane Goettel, Lisa Fay Coutley, and everyone at Black Lawrence Press for so very much. You all took a chance on my weird, little chapbook and believed in it. Lisa Fay Coutley is simply amazing. She (via email and phone) holds my hand. She keeps me honest. She's funny as hell and makes me want to be better than I am. And thank you to Zoe Norvell, who crafted a cover that should shine in the sky like a Batman light because it's so perfect.

Thank you Darcie Dennigan (again,) Jose Hernandez Diaz, and Ben Loory for reading *Horsemouth and Aquariumhead* and writing such nice things about it. I am still in awe that you three agreed to do so; I'm truly grateful.

Thank you Chris, Casey, and Thea. I am so so lucky to have you three.

ELIZABETH HORNER TURNER'S debut poetry chapbook, *The Tales of Flaxie Char*, was published through dancing girl press in 2017. Her work has been published widely in journals such as *Cutbank*, *Fairy Tale Review*, *Gulf Coast*, *Lost Balloon*, and *trampset*, and it has also been selected for inclusion in *Best Small Fictions* and *Wigleaf's* Top 50 and Long List. She's been awarded scholarships to Tin House Workshop and Sewanee Writers' Conference. She earned a BA from Hamilton College, an MFA from Sarah Lawrence College, and lives in San Francisco.

www.ingramcontent.com/pod-product-compliance
Lightning Source LLC
Chambersburg PA
CBHW050429110726
47899CB00008B/2909